This book belongs to:

_____

# The Secret of the First One Up

# The Secret of the First One Up

by Iris Hiskey Arno

*illustrated by* Renée Graef

NorthWord press
Chanhassen, Minnesota

The illustrations were created using airbrushed acrylic paint, colored pencil, and gouache
The text and display type were set in Minion and Janson Old Style
Composed in the United States of America
Designed by Lois A. Rainwater
Edited by Aimee Jackson

Books for Young Readers
NorthWord Press
18705 Lake Drive East
Chanhassen, MN 55317
www.northwordpress.com

Library of Congress Cataloging-in-Publication Data

Arno, Iris.
The secret of the first one up/by Iris Hiskey Arno; illustrations by Renée Graef.
p.   cm.
ISBN: 1-55971-867-6 (hc.)
[1. After a long winter's sleep, a young groundhog named Lila wakes up before anyone
else in her family, goes outside, and learns about her important role in predicting the
arrival of spring. Includes information on the American tradition of celebrating Groundhog
Day. 2. Woodchuck—Fiction. 3. Groundhog Day—Fiction.] I. Graef, Renée, ill. II. Title.

PZ7. H625Se 2003

[E]—dc21                                                                                          2002043112

Printed in Singapore
10  9  8  7  6  5  4  3  2  1

*For Max and Zack,*
*remembering fondly when they were the first ones up*

—I. H. A.

*To the wonderful teachers at*
*Westlawn Elementary School in Cedarburg, Wisconsin*

—R. G.

**L**ila twirled around and around in the candlelit den. On the wall, her shadow spun like a whirling top.

"Time for all groundhogs to be in bed!" Papa called.

"But I'm not tired!" Lila cried. "I can't possibly sleep all the way until spring!"

"Now, Lila," Mama said, "everyone else is in bed and Uncle Wilbur is about to head for his den."

Lila made a face at her drowsy brother and snoring sister and began to waltz with her shadow. She knew that Above Ground chilly winds shivered through the forest and fat gray squirrels scurried to check their hidden acorns. Down Below, her family was happy to climb into bed and pull fluffy covers under furry chins. Every one of them was ready for the long winter sleep. But not Lila.

"I hate to go to bed," she said. "It's such a long, long time until spring."

"That's how I used to feel when I was a young groundhog," Uncle Wilbur said. "But now I enjoy all the rest I can get."

"You always get up early to go Above Ground," Lila said. "What do you do up there? Aren't you scared to go all alone? Is it cold? Is it snowy? Is anyone else around? What do you do up there?"

"If I answered all your questions, I'd never get to sleep!" said Uncle Wilbur. "Even worse, I'd give away the secret."

"What secret?" Lila asked.

"The secret of the first one up," said her uncle.

"But I want to know!" said Lila. "I love secrets!"

"Then make sure you are up earlier than anyone else," said her uncle. "That's the only way to know. That's how it's always been and that's the fun of it."

He scooped Lila up, tucked her into bed and kissed her goodnight.

"See you in the spring," he said, tiptoeing out the door.

"But how will I know when to wake up?" Lila called after him.

Uncle Wilbur's voice echoed from the tunnel.

"Just . . . try . . . to . . . beat . . . me!"

Lila listened to Papa's rumbling snore and Mama's deep, even breathing.
"I'm going to do it. I'm going to be the first one up," she said, yawning.
"But the only way to be sure is not to go to sleep at all." She rubbed her eyes
and yawned again. "I'll think of exciting things like digging new tunnels and
running through the forest and mysterious secrets and . . ."

Then Lila was spinning. Down and down she spun into the warm darkness of a deep winter sleep.

Above Ground the days passed. Storms roared, branches snapped, snow fell and melted and fell again. Cardinals flashed red through the white landscape and perched on ice-covered branches. Deer wandered through the trees searching for food.

And then one day, Lila's eyes flew open. She leaped out of bed.

"Who's there? What happened?" she cried.

Nothing moved. No one was awake, but Lila knew from the smell of the air and the feel of the earth that a long time had passed since her Uncle Wilbur had tucked her into bed.

Uncle Wilbur! He had challenged her to be the first one up! But maybe he was already Above Ground and she would never learn the secret!

Lila pulled on her clothes and ran along the dark, silent tunnel.

"Uncle Wilbur, I woke up all by myself!" she called, poking her head into his den. She patted the sleeping bulge of blankets. "I beat you! What do you think of that?" Her uncle snored softly.

"Let's go Above Ground!" Lila cried. She shook his shoulder. "Come on! Let's go!"

"Not yet," he murmured, ". . . a few minutes more."

But Lila couldn't wait, not even for one more minute. She had to be out under the open sky, to breathe the wind blowing through the forest clearing and to hear the birds calling. She just had to know the secret!

Lila hurried up the tunnel toward the light. Bursting out into the open air, she found herself surrounded by those who stay awake all winter— squirrels, deer, beaver, foxes, rabbits, raccoons, cardinals, chickadees, badgers, and porcupines.

"Tell us! Tell us!" they cried. "Do you see it?"

Lila blinked in the bright light.

"See what?" she asked.

"Your shadow!" cried the animals. "Do you see your shadow?"

Was the secret about shadows? The animals stood watching her. No one moved. The clearing became so still that Lila's ears roared with the silence. She took a deep breath. The air felt cool and smelled piney and brand new.

Lila looked down at the ground, searching for the gray shadow that had danced with her in the candlelight. She looked to her left and then to her right. She twisted around and looked behind her.

Suddenly Lila felt lonely—the only groundhog awake without even her little shadow for company.

"I'm sorry," she said. "I don't see it."

"Don't be sorry!" the animals cried, dancing around the clearing. "Spring is coming!"

"Spring is coming?" Lila asked. "But how do you know?"

An old badger stopped his dance and peered at her curiously.

"My Uncle Wilbur said if I was the first one up, I would learn a secret," Lila said.

"Ah yes, the secret," said the old badger. "It's very simple. Every year, the first groundhog up on this day has the special job of looking for his or her shadow. If it's there, then there will be six more weeks of winter and the groundhog hurries back to bed."

"I would hate that!" Lila said.

"If, like today, the shadow isn't there," the old badger continued, "it means spring is coming and we all rejoice!"

"But you need the sun to have a shadow," said Lila. "So a beautiful sunny day means winter is staying and a cloudy gray day means spring is coming? That seems backwards to me!"

Just then, Lila heard a familiar voice behind her.

"Backwards it may be, but it's the way of shadows and spring!" said her uncle, climbing out of the tunnel.

"I did it, Uncle Wilbur! I did it!" she cried. "I was the first one up! And I learned the secret! And is it true about spring? Is it really coming?"

"Would all our neighbors wait for the first groundhog each year if we didn't do a good job of predicting spring?" Uncle Wilbur asked.

"If spring is coming, can we go Down Below and wake everyone up?" Lila asked. "Can we make some acorn pancakes and have a picnic to welcome spring?"

"My stomach is grumbling already," said her uncle.

Lila slipped her little paw into her uncle's big one.

"We won't tell anyone our secret, will we?" she asked.

"Of course not," said Uncle Wilbur, smiling down at her.

Lila smiled back. "Because that's how it's always been and that's the fun of it," she said.

# AUTHOR'S NOTE

SINCE THE LATE 1880s there has been an American tradition of celebrating Groundhog Day on February 2. On this day, tradition has it that the groundhog ends its winter sleep and comes above ground. If the day is sunny and the groundhog sees its shadow, there will be six more chilly weeks of winter. If the day is cloudy and the groundhog does not see its shadow, tradition says there will be an early spring. On this special day, therefore, bad weather brings good news.

This holiday was brought to the United States of America by people who left Germany and Great Britain and came across the ocean to live in the New World. In Germany, the badger was the animal to watch for a weather prediction, but somehow when the tradition crossed the Atlantic, the groundhog (also known as the woodchuck) took the badger's place.

Some cities have their own official groundhog and Groundhog Clubs. Sun Prairie, Wisconsin, has Jimmy the Groundhog. Punxatawney, Pennsylvania, calls itself "the original home of the great weather prognosticator, His Majesty the Punxatawney Groundhog." They celebrate the event from dawn to dusk in honor of their very own Punxatawney Phil, the "King of Weather Prophets."

Is the groundhog accurate in predicting spring? Why don't you watch and see what happens this year?

IRIS HISKEY ARNO began her career as a classical singer. She toured the U.S., Canada, and Europe singing opera, medieval, and contemporary music. When she became a mom, she took off her traveling shoes and started writing children's books. She also combined her interest in music with her interest in children's literature and wrote several musicals for children to perform. Iris lives with her husband and their two sons just outside New York City in a house with a rainbow-colored porch.

RENÉE GRAEF received her Bachelor's Degree in Art from the University of Wisconsin-Madison. She has illustrated over 40 children's books, including the Laura Ingalls Wilder series, and the "Kirsten" books and paper dolls from the American Girl Collection. Renée lives in Wisconsin with her husband and their two children.